Usborne
That's not my...
Things that go
Activity book

Find me on every double page.

Matthew Oldham

Illustrated by Rachel Wells

Designed by Josephine Thompson,
Eleanor Stevenson, Hannah Ahmed & Mary Cartwright

Based on the Usborne touchy-feely That's not my... series.

Spot the differences between these scenes.
There are THREE to find.

That's my plane

Decorate your plane's wings.

Draw more fluffy clouds.

Who is looping the loop?

Can you find the little white mouse?

ZOOM!

How many birds can you spot?

That's my train

Fill in the missing loads.

Count the doors... 1... 2... 3.

CLICKETY-CLACK

Which door is the odd one out?

Draw some steam.

CHOO-CHOOO!

Little white mouse, where are you?

CLICKETY-CLACK

Can you make a train sound?

That's my dump truck

Can you spot a GREEN bird?

Where is the little white mouse?

Fill in the sand your dump truck is unloading.

Finish shading both trucks.

That's my tractor

Fill in the white parts to finish your tractor.

Can you find the little white mouse?

MOO!

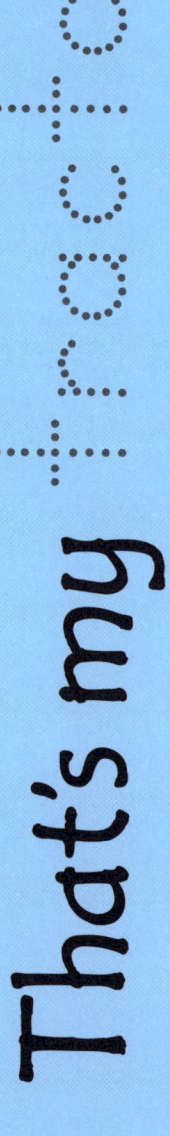

Fill in the smoke.

Can you chug like a tractor? CHUGGA-CHUGGA!

Which sheep is the odd one out?

Who's hiding in the grass?

That's my boat

Decorate your boat.

Can you see the little white mouse?

It's choppy out here!

Draw more choppy waves.

Find two sailing boats that MATCH.

Can you spot a YELLOW fish?

Look out for sharks! Can you see one?

That's my fire engine

Where is the little white mouse?

Fill in the white to finish your fire engine.

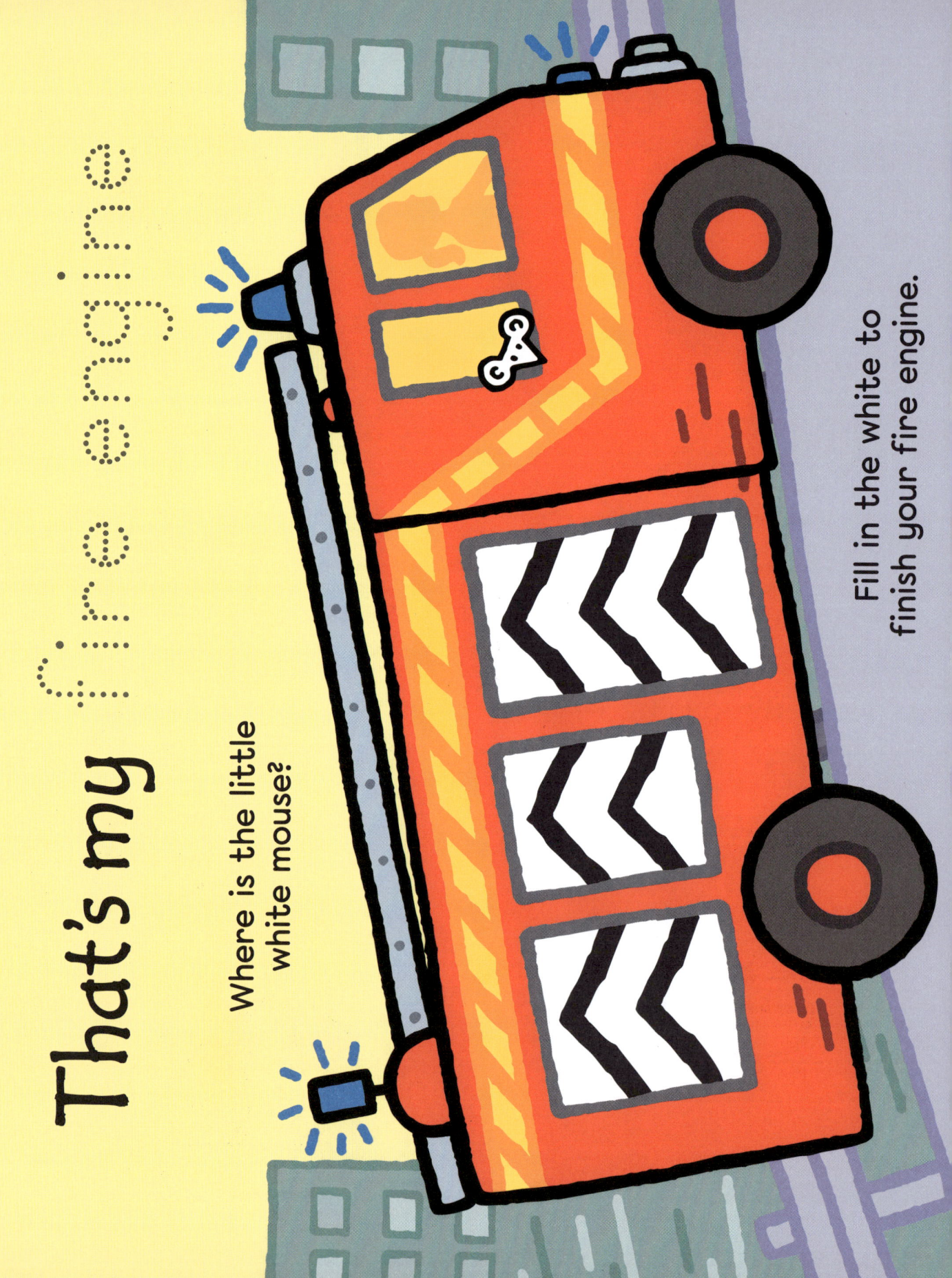

That's my car

Can you see the little white mouse?

Fill in the rest of your car.

Spot the differences between these blue cars.
There are THREE to find.

That's my digger

Can you help your digger to dig? Fill in what's in the scoop – and the hole it has made.

Little white mouse, where are you?

Can you see a RAINBOW?

Spot the differences in the pictures above.
There are FOUR to find.

That's my truck

Fill in the side of your truck.

Follow the road back, to see where your truck started.

22

Can you find the little white mouse?

Count ALL the sheep...
1... 2... 3... 4... 5.

That's my bike

Join the dots to finish your bike.

Where is the little white mouse?

Can you see a wriggly caterpillar?

I'm a worm.

24

Can you see another bike like THIS one?

Which bikes have baskets?

This ISN'T a bike...

It's a SCOOTER.
Fill in the wheels.

On the road

Find another car like this one.

BEEP! BEEP!

Can you see the little white mouse?

Find a WHITE TRUCK and fill it in.

Finish the lines in the road.

Where's my bus?

Who is NOT a mouse?

Eek eek!

Can you SQUEAK like a mouse?

Can you see a PINK parachute?

Goodbye!